"It was an army without guns,
but not without strength. . . ."
—Dr. Martin Luther King, Jr., 1964

THIS IS THE DREAM

BY DIANE Z. SHORE & JESSICA ALEXANDER

ILLUSTRATED BY JAMES RANSOME

Amistad

HarperCollins *Publishers*

These are the fountains
that stand in the square,
and the black-and-white signs
say who will drink where.

These are the buses—a dime buys a ride,

COLORED

but the people are sorted by color inside.

These are the restaurants where "WHITES ONLY" eat

FOR
COLORED
ONLY

WHITE ONLY
LADIES
REST ROOM

FOR COLORED PEOPLE

Pie
20¢

at tables up front and at lunch-counter seats.

These are the libraries, two separate sections,

with separate bookcases and separate selections.

These are the doors that are closed in the schools,
and "separate but equal" is not just a rule
but a law that's enforced on the buses and trains
and in theaters, rest rooms, department-store chains,

and in libraries, hospitals—*all* public places,
dividing up people by colors and races
with harsh written words that are slapped on the walls,
denying both freedom and justice for all.

These are the students who step through the doors

where people of color have not walked before.

These are the passengers, on weary feet,

walking until they can choose their own seat.

These are the diners who sit and who wait

at the "WHITES ONLY" counter, ignoring the hate.

These are the marchers who forge through the street

as they carry their message through shimmering heat.

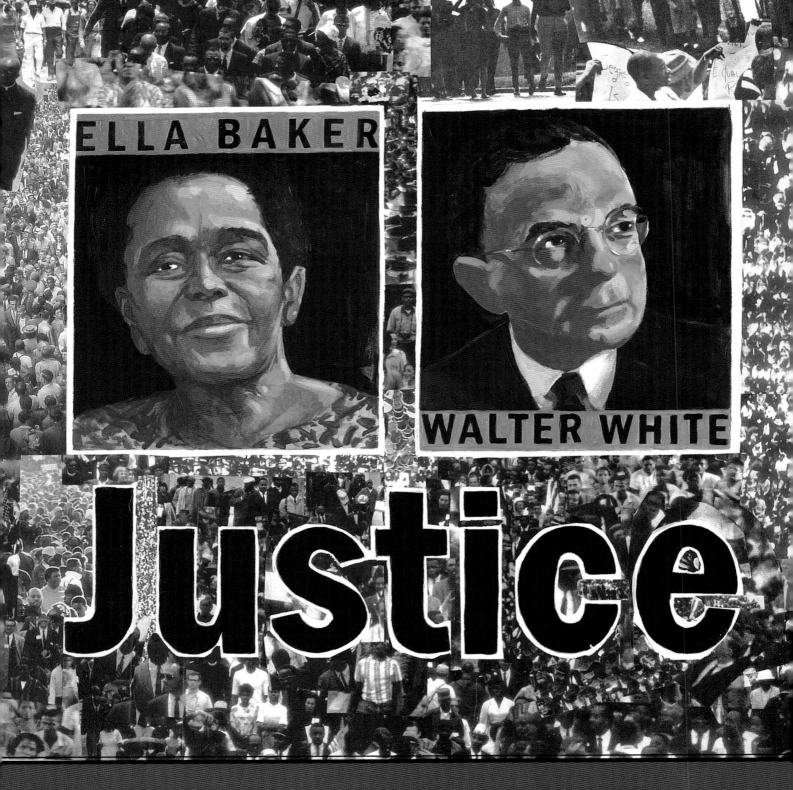

ELLA BAKER

WALTER WHITE

Justice

These are the leaders whose powerful voices
lift up the marchers demanding new choices
for fair-paying jobs and a good education,
to vote without fear and to live in a nation

THURGOOD MARSHALL

DR. MARTIN LUTHER KING, JR.

for all

where everyone's equal and judged from within,
never jailed or arrested because of their skin;
fighting firm without fists, sitting down, standing tall,
pressing onward toward freedom and justice for all.

This is the fountain that stands in the square,

and the unwritten rule is to take turns and share.

This is the bus that roars through the streets,

and all of the passengers choose their own seats.

This is the restaurant where, up in the front,

the black-and-white sign says **"OPEN FOR LUNCH."**

This is the library, books wall to wall

free to be read—not by some but by all.

This is the school where the doors open wide,
and the children are learning together inside
about students and marchers and leaders who fought
to make right what was wrong. Without violence they sought
to make changes together, establish new laws.

With many small triumphs they strengthened their cause
as they sat at the counters and rode through the stations
and gathered up hands as they marched through the nation;
with courage they rallied and answered the call . . .
dreaming of freedom and justice for all.

To Mom and Dad, who encourage me to follow my dreams.
—D.Z.S.

To Siobhan, Danica, Jacob, and Clee—may you rise and live bravely.
—J.A.

In memory of my childhood friend Darian Thomas Spruill, who introduced
me to *Mad* magazine. I'll never forget him.
—J.R.

A NOTE FROM THE AUTHORS

This Is the Dream celebrates the power of nonviolent change. It is a simple look at the way some things used to be, the steps that ordinary people took to change those things, and the way they are today in America. The journey is not over, however: Imperfections and inequalities remain in our society, and there is always room in our world for the kind of bravery that takes nonviolent action to create a better place. May this book be a testament to the courage of those who did and, above all, to peace.

D.Z.S. & J.A.

A NOTE FROM THE ILLUSTRATOR

I would first like to thank the writers, Diane Z. Shore and Jessica Alexander, for rising to the challenge of creating a lyrical manuscript that spans the years of the civil rights movement through the present day.

Growing up in the segregated South of the 1960s, I came to this project with some personal experience. I witnessed desegregation in the fifth grade, when in my town the all-black school merged with the all-white school. Some of my earliest memories are visiting the doctor's office with my grandmother and silently wondering why we were separated from people in the *other* waiting room. It wasn't until I got older that I realized the significance of this separation.

As I was growing up, I often saw the searing film clips and photographs from the civil rights movement, and I knew I somehow wanted to incorporate those images into *This Is the Dream*. The idea came to me of using collage to convey the emotion those early images evoked in me. This project also gave me the opportunity to take a closer look at the works of two of my favorite artists, Romare Bearden and Robert Rauschenberg, whose works greatly influenced the decorative collages.

I hope the combination of painting and collage will help the reader understand the emotional impact of the era, which can often be lost in reflections of the past. And most importantly, I hope this book touches the hearts of children and conveys the beauty of a time when relationships can blossom between many diverse cultures.

—J.R.

PHOTO CREDITS

Dan Weiner, courtesy of Sandra Weiner: pages 8 (far left, far right), 9 (far left) • Library of Congress: page 8 (middle, bottom) • Don Cravens: page 9 (far right) • © Flip Schulke: pages 10 (far left), 16, 17, 20 (far left), back jacket flap • © Bob Adelman/Magnum Photos: pages 16, 17, 20 (far right), 21 (all), back jacket flap • Associated Press: page 16 (middle) • Charles Moore/Black Star: pages 16 (middle), 17 (middle)